that
pesky
rat

lauren child

CANDLEWICK PRESS

Thank you
Randala

and for anyone
who has ever
wished they were
somebody's pet

Max

and
Albena

Sam

Louie

Lucy

Zaida

and for fabulous
Frances and her
pets Lucy, Sam,
Ata, and Cui

This book is for
the gorgeous Max
and her little
dog, Louie

Flame

Sita

Twinkle

with love to Jo and Thomas,
long-suffering owners of Twinkle,
the Bette Davis of cats

Ata & Cui

Cheeky

First U.S. paperback edition
2014
First published in
Great Britain in
2002 by Orchard Books,
London
Library of Congress
Catalog Card Number
2001058106

ISBN 978-0-7636-7298-0
WKT 18 17 16 15 14 13
10 9 8 7 6 5 4 3 2 1
Printed in Shenzhen, Guangdong, China
Candlewick Press
99 Dover Street
Somerville, Massachusetts 02144
visit us at www.candlewick.com

Donut

This is me.
I'm the one with the **pointy** nose and b e a d y eyes.
The cutesy one in the middle.

I live in trash can number **3**, **Grubby** Alley.

Every now and then I come back to find that someone has emptied **all my belongings** into a **big** truck and driven off with them.

It's very **upsetting**.

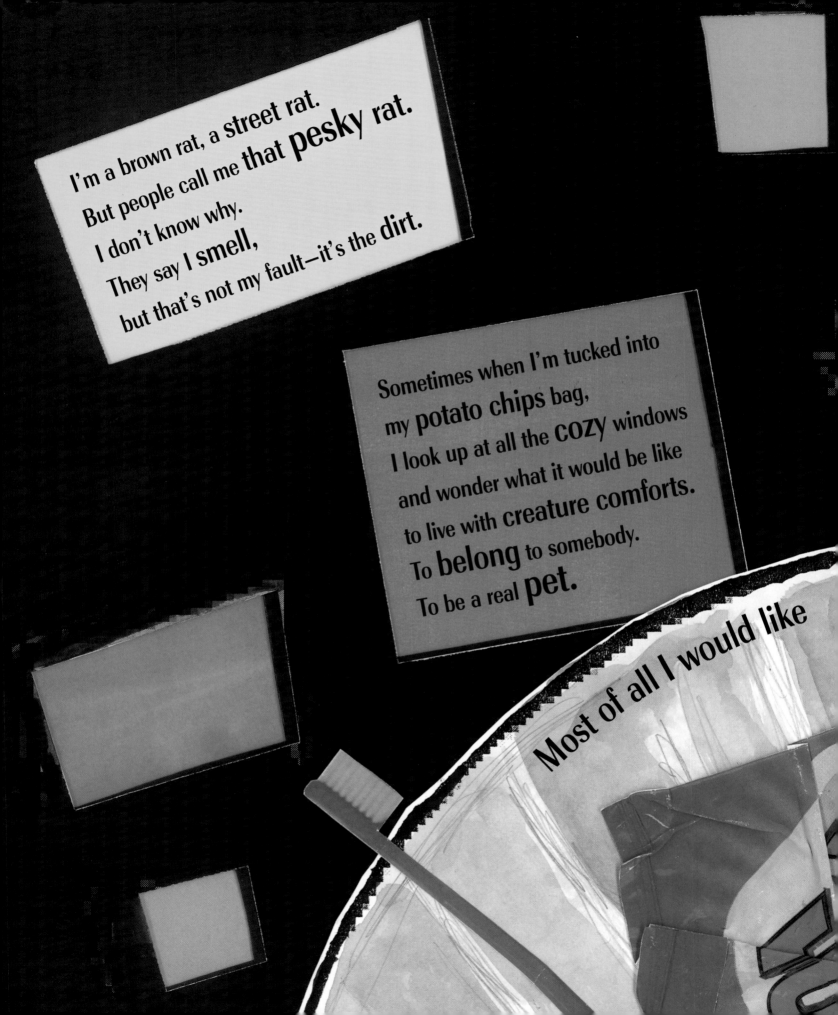

I'm a brown rat, a street rat.
But people call me that **pesky rat.**
I don't know why.
They say I **smell,**
but that's not my fault—it's the **dirt.**

Sometimes when I'm tucked into
my **potato chips** bag,
I look up at all the **cozy** windows
and wonder what it would be like
to live with **creature comforts.**
To **belong** to somebody.
To be a real **pet.**

Most of all I would like

My friend Pierre,

who is a **chinchilla**,

belongs to a lady named Madame Fifi.

He has a very **glamorous** life.

He lives in the lap of **luxury**.

I say, "I sure would like to live in a fashionable apartment and be fed chocolates while I sit on a feather cushion."

I hate taking baths.

I think I'm **allergic** to soap.

Then there's this **Siamese** cat named **Oscar**.
He lives with **Mr. Washington**, a **busy** businessman.

Mr. Washington is **always** at **work**, so he doesn't have time to **wash fur** or be **strict**.

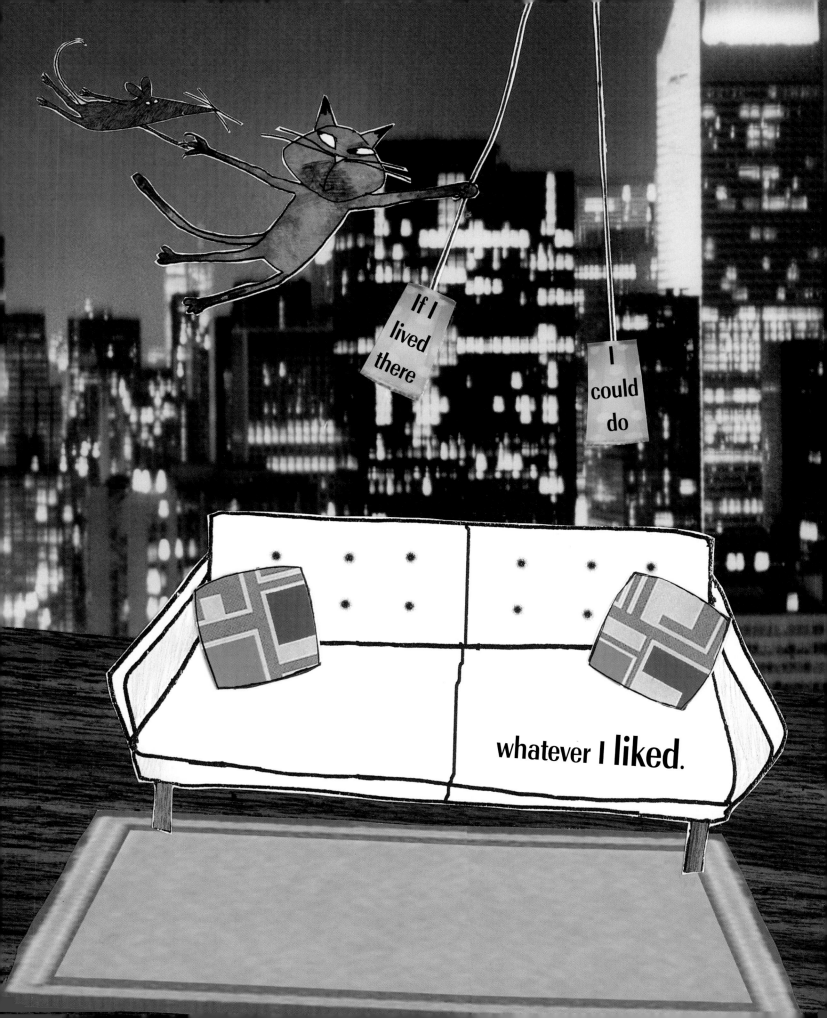

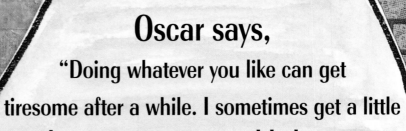

Oscar says,
"Doing whatever you like can get tiresome after a while. I sometimes get a little **bored** watching the **same old shows** on TV.

I even have to get my own supper."

I'm very good in the kitchen

but I hate

to be

b o r e d.

A **lop-eared** rabbit I know named **Nibbles** works in a **circus** with **Mr. HoOpla**. It must be so **exciting**— never a **dull** moment.

Swinging on the trapeze one minute, tiptoeing on the high wire the next.

Maybe it's all a little too nerve-wracking for me.

I think I'd really like one of those owners
who does a lot of **sitting around**—
like **Miss St.Clair.**

Her **Scottie** dog, Andrew, is **always** sitting by the

fire, having supper on a tray, and they spend the evenings doing Puzzles together.

Andrew says,

"On the whole I feel **very well** cared for.

And Miss St.Clair is good company.

But it's kind of **embarrassing** when we go shopping."

Miss St.Clair makes Andrew wear a little hat and coat.

I don't think **clothes** would suit **me.**

But I would do almost **anything** to be somebody's **pet.**

So in the morning
I go to the pet store
and ask Mrs. Trill

if she has

any customers

who might want me.

She says,

"There isn't much demand for brown rats. I'm afraid you aren't very **popular** with the public."

I say,

"I don't see why **not**. I'm very good **company**, always **popping up** when you least expect me to, and I'm happy to eat **anything**, even if it's been slightly **nibbled**."

Mrs. Trill says,

"Well, you could always hang a **notice** in the **window**. You never **know**."

So I write:

Me

Brown rat looking for kindly owner
with an interest in cheese
Hobbies include nibbling and chewing
would like a collar with my name on it
would like a name
would prefer no baths
will wear a sweater if pushed
Yours sincerely
Brown rat (that pesky rat)
P.S. Sorry about bad paw writing

not
a very good picture

Then I wait and I wait

and   I   wait.   Until . . .

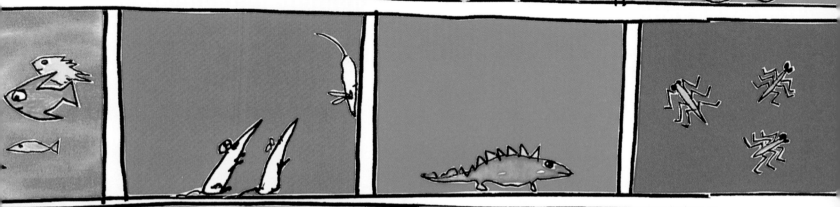

. . . on Tuesday old **Mr. Fortesque** walks by
and **stops** to look at my **notice.**

He really has to **squint** because he
has such **bad** eyesight.

Then he looks at me and says,

"My,
what a pointy
nose you have,
and, goodness me,
what a long tail, and such
unusual beady eyes . . .

I'll take him."

I can't
believe my **luck,**
and neither can Mrs. Trill.

Mrs. Trill says,
"Are you **sure**?"

And **Mr. Fortesque says,**
"Oh yes, I've been looking for a **brown cat**
as **nice** as this one for **ages.**"

Mrs. Trill looks at **me** and **I** look at Mrs. Trill,
and we **both** look at my notice,

but neither of us
says a **word.**

I just **love** being a **pet.**

And . . . I am trying to be **really** helpful.

I pick out the best **cheeses**

by using my excellent **sniffing nose.**

I clean the kitchen

by n i b b l i n g

up the

c r u m b s.

I help Mr. Fortesque

cross the **I** road by **scaring** the traffic.

And I'm **always** there when he comes **home**.

So here I am, a pet with a name.

So what
if I have to
wear a little
sweater?

Mr. Fortesque says, "Well, Tiddles, who's a pretty kittycat?"